W9-BRY-484

DARDED

E
TAY   Taylor, C.J.

         The Messenger of Spring

              02/99 $16.00

GI
       SCHOOL   RY

THE MESSENGER OF SPRING

GIBSONS ELEMENTARY
SCHOOL LIBRARY

For May, My heartfelt thanks

Copyright © 1997 by C.J. Taylor

Published in Canada by Tundra Books / *McClelland & Stewart Young Readers*,
481 University Avenue, Toronto, Ontario M5G 2E9

Published in the United States by Tundra Books of Northern New York,
P.O. Box 1030, Plattsburgh, New York 12901

Library of Congress Catalog Number: 97-60508

All rights reserved. The use of any part of this publication reproduced, transmitted in any form or by any means, electronic, mechanical, photocopying, recording, or otherwise, or stored in a retrieval system, without the prior written consent of the publisher - or, in case of photocopying or other reprographic copying, a licence from the Canadian Copyright Licensing Agency - is an infringement of the copyright law.

Canadian Cataloguing in Publication Data

Taylor, C. J. (Carrie J.),   1952-
        The messenger of spring

ISBN 0-88776-413-4

1. Ojibwa Indians – Folklore.   I. Title.

PS8589.A88173M47 1997   j398.2'089'973   C97-930708-2
PZ8.1.T36Me 1997

We acknowledge the support of the Canada Council for the Arts for our publishing program.

Printed and bound in Canada

1 2 3 4 5 6   02 01 00 99 98 97

THE MESSENGER
OF SPRING

C.J. Taylor

GIBSONS ELEMENTARY
SCHOOL LIBRARY

Tundra Books

The tattered wigwam sat beside a frozen stream. Iceman watched his campfire grow smaller and smaller. He thought of the days he made the snow drift into high banks. Now he was tired and old. Very, very old.

He heard a voice calling from across the stream. There stood a young stranger. Around his head he wore a wreath of sweetgrass. In his arms he carried a bunch of flowers. Where he walked, the snow melted away.

"Hello, Grandfather," called the stranger, "I bring you an important message. May I share your camp?"

"It is good to have company. It has been a long season," answered Iceman.

The stranger crossed the stream. Iceman heard the ice cracking and the water beginning to flow.

The young stranger sat beside the dying fire. Tiny green shoots of grass pushed up out of the earth all around him. Iceman poked at the flames with a stick.

"I am sorry my fire does not offer much comfort. I prefer the cold myself."

The stranger leaned forward and gently blew on the embers. Flames leapt high and bright. The blanket of snow that covered Iceman shrank away.

"My name is New Dawn," said the young stranger, "I bring an important message. But first, Grandfather, tell me of your power. I have heard many stories of your powers which are strong enough to change the earth."

New Dawn waited for Iceman to speak, but he was still for a long time. So still, New Dawn thought he had fallen asleep.

Suddenly Iceman began to speak, "There was a time when I was young and strong like you. When I commanded, the leaves fell from the trees and turned brown. My breath blew them away. I was so powerful, bears hid from me in their caves. Beavers dared not come out from their dams. Ducks and geese flew away to distant lands. Even the turtles and snakes hid in the mud."

"With a wave of my hand," Iceman slowly lifted his arm, "the ground turned as hard as rock. The waters became clear and as hard as crystal." Bowing his head he said, "But now, I am old and tired."

GIBSONS ELEMENTARY
SCHOOL LIBRARY

Iceman grew smaller and smaller as he spoke. "My strength was so great, I covered the earth with snow and ice. When I shook my head, snow blew into great drifts. I made the winds howl. It was so cold, people were afraid to leave their wigwams."

Drawing in a long slow breath, Iceman shook his head with all his might. Only a few large snowflakes floated down. New Dawn saw tears in his eyes. His voice was weak.

"I am old and tired," said Iceman, "Now you must tell me of this message you bring."

New Dawn stood up and began to sing. He grew very tall. There was a flash of lightning. A soft rain fell. The vale of snow that had covered the earth began to melt away.

New Dawn stood high above the treetops. The sky grew brighter, and he sang louder. The branches stretched toward the warm sun. Swelling buds burst open, filling the branches with bright new leaves.

Songbirds gathered around New Dawn. Swallows, chickadees and bluebirds flew and hopped about. Waxwings, grosbeaks, robins and red-winged blackbirds joined in song. The woods and meadows were filled with sound. As the sun rose to the center of the sky, the earth grew warmer.

New Dawn began to dance, his feet softly touching the earth. The animals woke from their winter sleep. Bears came out of their caves looking for food. Turtles crawled out of their muddy homes. Snakes sunned themselves on rocks. Tiny green shoots of grass covered the forest floor. Caterpillars feasted on fresh new leaves.

New Dawn sang louder as he continued to dance. His song called back the waterfowl. The swamps and marshes were alive. Herons lined the shores. Ducks searched for places to build their nests. Geese honked their greetings as they flew overhead.

A warm breeze swept across the earth, carrying New Dawn's song. Soon the woods were filled with birds busy feeding their chicks. Mother rabbits watched their young nibble on new leaves. Curious fawns explored as their mothers kept careful watch. Insects found suitable places to build their homes. Bears and their cubs romped through the meadows looking for berries. The earth that was once covered with snow and ice was now filled with color, scent and sound.

New Dawn ended his song. He turned towards Iceman's camp. Where his wigwam once stood remained only decaying poles. Iceman was no longer there. In his fire pit, a beautiful white and pink flower, the wild portulaca or 'Spring Beauty,' grew in the middle of the dead embers.

New Dawn heard Iceman's voice. "Your power is great. You have brought color and life to the earth. I leave you this gift; it brings beauty and the first food of the season. At its roots grows a bulb. It is good to eat. The earth will know your power is greater than mine when this 'Spring Beauty' first appears. Goodbye my young my friend, until we meet again."

New Dawn gave thanks to Iceman for his wonderful gift. He could hear the voices of women and children filling the woods with laughter. Gathering the flowers and roots, they, too, gave thanks for Iceman's gift and for the dawn of a new season and all that it brings.

DISCARDED